THE LITTLE DOG

IN THE

BIG PLAGUE

C.C. ALMA

ALSO BY C.C. ALMA

The Earth Girl and Queen Eliza

This novella is included in
Stories in the Okay Future, an anthology of
short fiction by C.C. Alma.

Part I

Ringo's sense of smell was powerful, even for a dog, but that wasn't his only talent. He was also sensitive to the energies emanating from other live bodies, especially those from his human family.

Lately, he could sense that Aunt Charlene's body had changed. She had been getting heavier, and now there was extra sugar in her bodily liquids. Ringo could smell it in the bathroom after she urinated. Some humans smelled like that, and now Aunt Charlene was one of them.

She had been struggling with her energy and her moods. She was a quiet woman with a pleasant demeanor, but that was only on the outside. Ringo knew that she had been worried and stressed, but he also knew that things had been getting better since the family started their evening walks. Aunt Charlene was walking at a slower pace due to some pain and stiffness in her feet; even so, her mental and physical states were slowly improving.

Emmy, the little girl, had much more energy, but she slowed her pace to match with her aunt and her dog. She was calm and sweet, like her guardian aunt, and she understood that these walks were a time for Auntie to get healthier.

Ringo didn't understand the dogs and the humans that jogged by, looking tense and determined. It was awful for some of those dogs, and Ringo was happy he was not one of them. Aunt Charlene, Emmy, and Ringo moved through their environments at a leisurely pace. They were a well-matched group of personalities, and they made a great team. They were a reserved and cautious group, but appreciative of every detail there was to notice and observe.

Some of the people in the neighborhood didn't like Ringo that much. They tensed in his presence, or they made a face. Other dogs got petted and cooed at, but that didn't happen often with Ringo. He didn't understand this, and he didn't care. Humans could be weird sometimes. And strangers invading his family? Not cool. He figured that they saw him as the guardian and protector of a vulnerable woman and child.

These were good times. Ringo loved exploring the neighborhood. Even though they often took the same route, there was always something different to see and smell. There were new dandelions on some lawns, new markings from other dogs, and each day the leaves on the tree branches were a little more unfurled, a little larger. It was a beautiful, fragrant neighborhood.

Except for *that smell*. There was something in the air that Ringo could no longer ignore, and he was getting concerned.

It had started a few weeks ago. It had been faint, like the smokestacks from a distant city that had wafted over, just a bit, or like a faint rotting smell from a faraway diseased forest. But every day the smell was getting stronger, and it was entering bodies and infecting them. People, dogs, cats, birds—they were all beginning to take it on.

Ringo thought that maybe they should move back to their old apartment complex, even though there weren't any nice paths for walking and that home was small. That area might be safe from the rot. Aunt Charlene and Emmy were clueless, though—they loved their new neighborhood and their big new house.

Ringo changed his mind about moving back when they visited their old neighbor, Mary Pat, and the smell was there, too. Mary Pat was a nice elderly lady and a good friend to the family, so Ringo was alarmed to notice that she reeked of this awful odor. He made sure to keep his body extra still when she petted him. She smelled so rotten that Ringo knew that she would soon feel sick. When they left Mary Pat's apartment, Ringo turned his head back into the doorway, stared at her, and whined. She seemed delighted at Ringo's behavior, but she didn't understand. Ringo was just sad for her, and he knew that he would probably never see her again.

Once they were in the car, Ringo pressed his nose into Aunt Charlene's neck and took a good whiff. Aunt Charlene laughed and pushed him away, but Ringo only grunted and pressed harder into her thick flesh. Then he sniffed Emmy's neck. Emmy patted Ringo's face and asked her aunt a question. Ringo heard his name; he knew they were wondering why his behavior was so odd. Aunt Charlene just shrugged. She was in good spirits, happy because her body was feeling lighter and stronger.

Ringo buried his head into Emmy and whimpered. He couldn't help it. He was so sad for them, but maybe it was

C.C. ALMA

better that they and everyone else in the city didn't know what lay ahead.

Aunt Charlene and Emmy were the two people he loved more than anyone else in the world, but he knew now that they had it. They had the disease.

* * *

Tobey loved playing the new video game with Serge, his cousin in the Philippines. They hadn't been in the same country since Tobey and his family visited the Philippines nearly ten years ago, but Tobey and Serge still played cyber games. They had always been perfectly matched—Tobey won half the games, Serge won the other half. They were improving their skills at a matched speed, although Serge had won three in a row, which drove Tobey crazy.

"Score!" Tobey yelled.

"Stop the game, Tubby. I want to talk to you."

Tobey tensed. He hated it when his father called him by his baby nickname.

"We're almost done," Tobey said.

"Stop the game. Now."

Oh no. There was *that* voice. Tobey had been hearing it a lot lately. Dad was in one of those moods, again, and Tobey knew it was now pick-a-fight time. It didn't seem to matter that Tobey was in the middle of something— whatever Dad was focusing on at the moment, everyone in the family had to stop their lives and focus on it too. Not fair. And because Dad was in a bad mood, Tobey had to drop his good time and bow down to the master.

Tobey stopped the game. Serge knew the drill, just like Tobey knew it when Serge disappeared when the girlfriend was around.

"Yes, Dad."

"How long have you been playing that damn game?"

"I don't know. A couple of hours."

"A couple of hours."

"That's what I said."

"What time is it?"

"The clock's on the mantle, if you want to know."

"It's 9:30 a.m. on a Tuesday morning. Do you know where most of the world is?"

"On the other side of the planet, they're probably in bed."

Tobey's father sighed. "They're at work. Just like I was at work. Now I'm going to bed. Because I work a graveyard shift. You know what that is, right? It's called a job. And I suffered through it, even though I've been sick. Your mother is sick, too. No one is feeling well except for you. But we go to work anyway. We pay our bills and we act like grownups."

Tobey said nothing. He wanted to say that maybe everyone was so sick because they all kept going to work and infecting everyone else. And that he *had* been looking for work. He'd contacted every damn place he could think of in Virginia Beach and every neighboring city in the area. He had even sent resumes to other states in case he could get a chance to leave it all behind: his nagging father, his silently disapproving mother, and his super-smart college student brother.

"How old are you?"

Tobey could feel the anger and frustration rising in him and about to explode. He glared at his father. He was twenty years old, twenty-one in two months. "You know how old I am! I've *tried*. I've contacted every office, hotel, restaurant, barbershop, post office, bus terminal, airport, data center, hospital, and store!"

"What about the Pickford Building? They're looking for security guards."

"And every damn place in the city," Tobey continued. "You know why I quit my last job. The boss was a jerk! He was touchy feely with all the waitresses, and they hated him. But they were mothers who needed the work, and they were scared. And he knew it. And when he found out that Elizabeth Jones was gay, he kept calling her Liz the Lez. And he thought that was funny. And he was always—"

"That was a year ago, Tubby."

Tobey stood up and faced down his father. Tobey was six feet, four inches, muscular but fleshy—he was slightly overweight, but his body could carry extra fat without looking too soft. Tobey often wondered if he had been adopted. His father and brother were five feet, ten inches, skinny, and prone to freckling. They had dark freckles on dark skin, chocolate flakes on caramel flan. Tobey was pale; he had cheeks that flushed when he got emotional. His face was red now, and his mop top of dark hair was damp with sweat.

Dad stared up at his looming son. The little old man had all the power, and Tobey knew it. Dad owned the house, let Tobey sleep in his childhood bed, fed him, bought his video games, and slipped him some cash when he was in better moods.

"I am sick. I need to rest," Tobey's father said as he turned toward the doorway. "And your brother said they're looking for cafeteria workers on his college campus."

He walked across the room, stomping angrily on the floor. His crackly old flip flops clicked back on his heels, sounding ridiculous. Didn't he buy those things at some stall in the Philippines ten years ago? Tobey realized that he never saw his father wear anything else at home. Every morning he walked in the door, sat on the couch, tugged off his shoes, rubbed his stinky old feet and shoved them into those flip flops. "House slippers," he always called them. God, that was irritating.

Tobey glared down at his father's small, ugly feet. Sweep floors in some college cafeteria while his brother hung out with his college buddies, eating pizza and talking about whatever pre-meds talked about? Did his father have no sensitivity or was that a deliberate dig?

"I'd be out of here by tomorrow if I could," Tobey shouted at his father's stiff back. "I know you want me gone. Hell, I want to be gone too! Give me a break! I been trying, I been trying!"

"I don't want you gone. I want you home and busy and working," his father said.

Working and living at home until he was thirty years old, like his cousin in Norfolk—pleasing everyone in the family until they approved of the appropriate wife. No way. Tobey had big dreams. He was going to get rich and speed away from of this boring city as soon as he could. In a black Lamborghini.

"Like I said—I been trying!" Tobey shouted.

Dad was down the hall, heading for his bedroom. He was having a coughing fit and muttering to himself in Tagalog. "*Subukan ang mas,*" his father said. *Try harder.*

Tobey plopped down on the couch as his anger began to subside and the usual fear and restlessness crept in. He cradled his head in his hands. He didn't want to be his father—he didn't want to spend twenty years of his life flipping burgers at the all-night diner, doing graveyard shifts because the pay was slightly better. But what was he going to do with the rest of his life?

* * *

The bad smell grew fast in Aunt Charlene and Emmy. Just two weeks after the visit with Mary Pat, they were too ill to get out of bed. It was early afternoon, too early for nap time and too late to be sleeping in. Even so, Aunt Charlene and Emmy each lay prone in their separate bedrooms. Aunt Charlene had the large bedroom with its own bathroom, recently decorated in beige and green; Emmy had a small pink and white room with a fluffy pink area rug next to her narrow bed.

Ringo wasn't allowed on the beds, but that didn't matter anymore—all the rules seemed to be gone now, thrown out, along with the rest of the life they once had. He had spent the day keeping vigil on his sick family, alternately checking on each room. Now it was Emmy's turn, and he decided that he would break the rule.

He jumped up on Emmy's bed, which wasn't easy because he was a small dog. Emmy didn't object. She didn't have the strength to say much; she wasn't moving and her breath drew in and out in a weak rattle. Ringo snuggled up to her hot, sweaty body. She smelled terrible, but the core of her life was there. Emmy opened her eyes and began to pet Ringo while mumbling soft, affectionate words.

Twenty minutes later, Ringo needed to check on Aunt Charlene. He jumped down from Emmy's bed and trotted over to Aunt Charlene's room. Luckily the door was ajar, but Ringo hesitated before pushing the door open. It was as if the heat from Aunt Charlene's body had pumped out into the entire room, and the rotting stench from her body was unbearable.

Ringo pushed through the door and stood facing the bed. This bed was taller than Emmy's bed, and he may not be able to jump up on it. Did it even matter? Would he even be able to help in such a horrible situation? Ringo began to bark, his voice reverberating through the quiet house and the quiet neighborhood. His legs began to shake. He was hungry, tired, frustrated, and scared. He knew that he was alone in this situation and that there was no one who could help. The whole neighborhood was sick, too, so what could other humans do? He might not be able to be of service! Ringo barked louder.

"Hey, Ringo," Emmy said as she appeared in the bedroom doorway. "You be a good boy." She scooped him up and climbed into her aunt's bed.

Aunt Charlene held out her arms, and Emmy and Ringo snuggled in. Ringo kept his body still and tried his best to put out waves of emotional support. He wanted to be a good boy, like Emmy said. It was difficult work, but Ringo knew that he had to do it.

* * *

Three days passed, and Ringo no longer knew what to do. He sat on the front stoop of the house and stared out at the street. It was a warm and sunny morning, and big clouds hung in the sky. The rotting smell in the air had cleared out, just a little; the usual smell of car exhaust had been clearing away as well.

If Aunt Charlene and Emmy were alive, they would probably all go for a walk later that day, once the air cooled and the clouds became dark and pierced with thin strips of light. There would be no more family walks. Aunt Charlene and Emmy were still in Charlene's big bed, but the smell of life had drained away. Ringo had smelled the finality of it—their blood and lungs were no longer moving, and the outside forces were beginning to invade.

A truck was parked across the street. Ringo had been watching as a team of men carried out dead bodies from each house. He knew that they would reach his house at some point to take his family, and he was okay with that. He had said his goodbyes to Aunt Charlene and Emmy. Now it was time for their bodies to be processed by the other humans so that they could dissolve back into the earth in a proper manner.

A couple of women were walking by, chatting amiably. They were probably strangers seeking camaraderie and emotional support. Ringo could sense their grief but also their relief at having survived; but he knew that they were wrong—they would not survive. They had the smell.

"Hello, little poopsie," one of the women said to Ringo. "Come! Come with me."

No. She was a pleasant woman, but Ringo could smell the rot. He turned and ran back into the house through his doggy door, then watched them through the window as they walked away. She seemed disappointed about Ringo's rejection, but he didn't care. If he were to join a new family, they had to be rot free.

After they had disappeared, he went back outside. He would walk the path he had taken with Aunt Charlene and Emmy, as a tribute to their lives. He decided to walk that route every day, day after day, until he figured out what to do next.

THE LITTLE DOG IN THE BIG PLAGUE

* * *

Ringo had been walking the route continuously for a few days. He had eaten garbage, weeds, and parts of a freshly dead bird that smelled disease-free. He found a weeping willow tree that he liked, so he lay in its shade on the hot afternoons. It was a healthy, kind-hearted tree, and Ringo felt its welcoming hug when he was inside those soft curtains of leaves.

One morning, he circled back home to find the front door propped open and the bodies gone. Someone had painted a mark on the house. The smell of the paint made Ringo nauseous, so he left.

He wasn't sure if there was a need to go back. He felt heavy, stiff, and thirsty for clean, tasty water. He was frightened and lonely. He would miss Aunt Charlene and Emmy forever, but there must be some healthy humans who needed him. He decided to leave the route to go and find them.

* * *

The blonde man was handsome, but he had that rotted smell. He was newly infected with it, though, and he probably wouldn't die for a while. He was gesturing to Ringo and speaking in friendly tones. Ringo was coming forward, although he felt cautious.

The man smelled bad and appeared unhealthy, but not just in that diseased way. Ringo had an ability to detect different types of human souls. He knew that some dogs didn't have it; this was Ringo's special natural talent. He used to see a certain curly-haired dog walking with her person, and he would wonder why she was so happy and trusting. The curly-haired dog was clueless, in Ringo's opinion, because her person was so cold and blank. People like that should be avoided; they went through life just pretending to be pleasant and caring, but they were not.

Then there were the really good people, the best people, the ones who were so full of love and kindness that Ringo could feel that their bodies were both dappled with sunshine and damp with holy water, as if a seed of goodness within was being continually watered by a mysterious force of nature. These people had positive energies that radiated into the air, making other people feel good just being nearby. Ringo had encountered this a few times, but it was rare.

The vast majority of people were not like either one of these. Most people had that seed, but it was not well nourished. They had a lot of emotional hormones and changing moods; but they knew what goodness was, and they tried to be good. Aunt Charlene and Emmy were like this. These were the kinds of people that a dog could work for. All that complicated struggling that most humans experienced sometimes resulted in behavior that a dog should just ignore or forgive.

Ringo's usual talented instincts would have known that this was not a man he should take on, but he was beginning to feel desperate for a family. Despite the man's contracted, hollow energy, Ringo thought that maybe this man could be okay.

Ringo just felt so lost without his family. Aunt Charlene had managed their lives with a motherly wisdom that Ringo could not seem to create on his own. They had a daily schedule: a morning walk followed by a rawhide chew, then an evening walk followed by dinner. Ringo missed it all so much—the regular walks and the regular meals, play time, nap time, and snacks, all doled out to him in careful rations. Now he was eating whenever he found food that smelled edible, and he was feeling heavy and tired. He needed Aunt Charlene. This man might be okay.

Ringo came forward to see what the blonde man wanted. Was that food in his outstretched hand? It was. He appeared to be offering a dark and shiny strip of food that smelled like meat. Ringo gently took the strip from the man's hand. It was rubbery and meat-flavored, but so hard to chew that he wasn't sure what to do. Ringo wanted to show the man that he appreciated his offering, so he tried to consume it. It was a long piece of food, though, and as Ringo swallowed, he could feel part of it snaking down his throat while the other half of it remained stuck in his mouth.

Ringo started to sputter and choke. The man started to laugh, a delighted guffaw that made Ringo uncomfortable. The man leaned his face into Ringo's face, talking and laughing while Ringo choked down the food and eventually ingested it.

Water? Ringo needed it badly, not the murky stuff in the puddles, but fresh, tasty water like what Aunt Charlene used to provide. He looked questioningly at his new friend.

The man reached down. Ringo lowered his head, grateful for the attention. He had not been petted in a long time, and it was something that he had always enjoyed. The man laughed again, a single shout of sheer glee that didn't quite sound human. Ringo looked up, alarmed. Then the man's two hands came around Ringo's throat. The man began to grip, harder and harder. He squeezed and twisted Ringo's neck like someone wringing out a small rag.

* * *

Tobey had pierced a tall shovel into the middle of the front lawn. From the kitchen window, Tobey thought it looked like a flag that was claiming land for a pioneer homesteader—he had seen something like this in a historical documentary. Now that 95% of the world population was dead, he and the other survivors might go back to those days. Who knew? He just had to deal with today.

He was sitting in the kitchen, looking out at his shovel, and eating a sandwich. He had a big task ahead, so he had to take a break and gear up for it. It had been a harrowing night, and Tobey was exhausted. "Rest," his father had whispered from his deathbed. Rest, eat, drink, and then carry on. Carry on to what, Tobey wondered. They were all gone. Not gone. Dead.

Dead, dead, dead. And the backyard just wouldn't do for the burial. Tobey's mother had converted their small backyard into a large rose garden, and Tobey was not about to bury his mother, father, and brother among all those thorns. Who cared if he dug three big holes in the front yard, anyway? Everyone on this street was dead and waiting to be carted away by the men in uniform.

To hell with that. Tobey was not going to let his family get thrown into a big pit with all the other corpses. They were going to stay right here at home, where Tobey could always know where they were, even if he left home to go live out his life somewhere else. He might not even survive this plague. He was feeling tired and sore, so maybe he would die soon, too, and go join everyone else at the party in the sky.

What a month it had been. Not even a month. Tobey's father and mother had come down the sniffles; within a week they had been in bed, feverish, sweaty, and unable to eat, drink, or speak. Tobey's brother, Tom, had said that he would be coming home to help. "I've been studying all the reports," he had said—as if a twenty-two year-old pre-med student would have the answers to what mystified every medical expert on TV, some of them talking through plugged noses and congested lungs. As soon as Tobey had seen Tom's swollen and sweaty face, he knew that Tom could not help. So Tobey had shut off the TV. He didn't need to hear the 24/7 coverage about the world-wide pandemic, he just needed to deal with his world.

They had not been "I love you" type of family. Tobey had only heard those words from Tom, when Tom used to sneak home from parties, drunk and with a face covered in lipstick smears. Tom had been the smart, popular teenager. He had ignored Tobey at school, but he had helped Tobey with his homework at home, patiently explaining the math and chemistry concepts that Tobey had struggled to grasp. Dad had never said those three words. He was a "get a job" type of guy. Get a job, take some classes, go figure out life. Don't be like me. Mom was a "say your prayers" type of mom, and she was the only affectionate person in the family. She hugged and kissed her little boys every day; when they grew older, she acted as if her teenage sons were the most fascinating conversationalists in the world. She listened to every rambling story and giggled at every bad joke. She could talk about sports like no woman Tom and Tobey ever knew. Yes, Mom loved her boys. When Tobey struggled in the years after high school, she stayed quiet while Dad did all the pushing. That was Dad's way of showing he cared. Yes, there was love in the family.

A week ago, they had skin that looked bumpy, lined, and bruised—as if an incompetent tattoo artist had drawn the surface of the moon into their bodies. The damage was everywhere. And they had severe flu-like symptoms—they had been hot, sweaty, weak, and disoriented; but the bruised up, black and blue lines on their bodies had alarmed Tobey the most.

They had all died within hours of each other in a single morning. Mom had gone first, followed by Tom, then Dad. Tobey had spent hours and hours that night wiping down each body with cool towels. He had not been sure if it would help, but he had not known what else to do. The coolness seemed to reduce their tossing and turning, and they appeared to relax, just a little. Then it started all over again.

Towards the end of his life, Tobey's father had paused look intently at Tobey, as if he wanted to speak. "Stop and rest, Big Toe," Dad had whispered. "Eat something. It will be all right."

Big Toe. That was Tobey's other nickname, the cutesy one they had started in school that his brother and parents had picked up. Tobey didn't love it, but he didn't hate it. He knew he was a big dude with big feet—the dude who didn't say much in class, who struggled to keep up his C average, and who got cut from the basketball team because he was too slow and clumsy. What kind of six foot four guy gets cut from the basketball team? He did. So yeah, Big Toe, that was him. The big guy who was, in reality, a small, powerless, unemployed guy. Stop and rest, Big Toe, take a break, and pour some expired milk into a glass with your big shaky hands. Force down a baloney sandwich before you continue dealing with the big nightmare, a nightmare so huge that Big Toe felt like a little insect hunkering down in a category five hurricane.

And now—time to bury. Tobey felt the tears in his body, but they weren't up in his face. Somewhere inside him there were loud and ugly wails of frustration and grief; but they were dulled down, for now. He had a job to do. He could cry later, for the rest of his life, and it would probably be a short grieving time, anyway, to be ended when the evil virus killed him too. No crying. He had to deal with the situation. His family needed to be buried. Tobey got up and headed out the front door.

* * *

"Uggy AH! Hug Ah!" Ringo was sputtering out weak, ugly noises as he fought to take in air.

Is this what drowning felt like? Ringo had once been dunked under water and held down by a little bully boy. That had been terrifying. This was painful as well as terrifying. His body was zoned in on nothing but the pain in his neck—the world was fading away from Ringo's vision, sounds were growing faint, and smells were tunneling away into nothingness.

Ringo kept fighting and struggling through it all. He was fighting to take in air and fighting to burst away from the man's grip, but he just couldn't do it. And the man wouldn't quit—his hands twisted Ringo's neck like Aunt Charlene would an old rag. Squeeze, shake, then hang it up, tattered and limp and still a little dirty. Aunt Charlene! Where was she? Aunt Charlene had pushed the boy away and rescued Ringo from that horrifying drowning. She did it with a hotly intense energy that Ringo had never felt from her before. Aunt Charlene! As Ringo fought and flailed, the man's hands pressed in yet even more, with a strength and increasing firmness that Ringo did not think was possible.

Thoughts were firing off in Ringo's brain as he felt himself getting closer to death. Maybe it was okay—maybe it was meant to be, since Aunt Charlene and Emmy were now gone. Ringo had no one to work for now; he had certainly made a big mistake by trusting this cruel man. Ringo realized that he should have relied on his instincts and stayed away. It was too late.

Ringo could feel cold spikes of energy that were shooting out from the man's soul, brutal and vicious—it was too much. It was just too much. Ringo felt as if his eyeballs might pop out of his head and shoot into the sky. His tongue was sticking out, yet his teeth were biting in, and he could taste his own blood.

"Aaaaarg!" Ringo wailed.

The man let go. Ringo stumbled to the ground, disoriented, but he knew enough to run. And so he ran, as fast as he could. He could hear the man laughing as he sprinted further and further away. The man wasn't chasing Ringo—that was a relief—and as Ringo ran on, the man's hollow, wild laughter faded in the distance. Ringo didn't stop until the man's voice faded into silence.

* * *

It had been a harrowing morning; but as the day went on, Ringo began to relax, just a little. He spent the afternoon in the shade of the kindly weeping willow tree, but he scurried into the bushes when the occasional person walked by.

Ringo was feeling wary and lost. He was scared of most people now; they had unpredictable moods and rotting bodies. He needed at least one good person, a protector from the others, someone who could give him food and water. More than that, he wanted a new family of healthy people. They might not exist in this new world, and that was frightening.

Ringo could hear someone in the distance. A man was out doing some kind of yard work, moving around with rapid efficiency and muttering to himself. Ringo lifted his nose into a small breeze. Yes. He was a couple of blocks away—young, male, healthy. He had none of that rot. Ringo stood up and followed the scent.

* * *

Ringo sat in an alert, attentive position at a respectable distance, on the sidewalk, so that the man could have room to work. He was digging big holes in the front yard while three dead bodies lay on the front porch. Ringo assumed that the man was burying his family and that each body would get a separate hole. Ringo approved of this. The man had lost his family, just like Ringo had lost his, and he was putting in an effort to return their bodies to the earth.

The man was dirty and sweaty, and there were agitated waves of tension, anger, and sadness swirling around him. That was good, from Ringo's point of view. Emotion at this time was normal and good. Even more, he had that seed of decency—maybe just a tiny bit of it, but it was there, Ringo was sure of it. This man was healthy, and there was a good soul in him.

The young man ignored Ringo as he worked. That was okay, in Ringo's mind. Ringo would be patient; he would wait for the man to finish his project.

The man turned and faced Ringo. "Go away," he yelled. "Get!"

Ringo understood this, but he refused. He would wait.

It was getting hot, and Ringo was beginning to feel weak. His tummy and neck still hurt, and he needed some shade and a nap, but he continued to sit upright and watch the man admiringly. The next shady lawn was a few houses down, but Ringo did not want to move. This was his next person, and he had to keep him in sight.

The man must be tired, even though he kept on working at the same furious pace. Ringo was concerned—the man needed a break, but he wouldn't stop. Ringo stood up and came forward, wagging his tail. It was time that they were introduced. The man turned to Ringo and yelled. He was so upset and angry that Ringo backed away tentatively. He would give the man more time.

This seemed to irritate the man more. He picked up a pebble and tossed it at Ringo, hitting Ringo in his rump with a gentle ping. Ringo yelped. His skin had become tender from the hot sun, and the pebble stung more than he'd expected. He was still sore from the bad man—this act of dismissive annoyance was too much. He thought this man was good! That was enough. Ringo turned and began to trot away, whimpering softly and feeling ashamed. Aunt Charlene and Emmy had never liked it when Ringo acted timid. They encouraged him to project confidence, but that was not one of his strengths.

The man began following Ringo. Oh no. Ringo began to run as fast as he could. His four little legs were running faster than the big man's two legs, which Ringo found surprising. Keep going—he got away once, he could do it again. The man was screaming at Ringo as Ringo ran on, and Ringo kept on running.

Then Ringo heard a word he knew. "Sorry," the man was saying. "Sorry, sorry, sorry!" That was the word that Emmy had used when she ran around too fast and then stepped on Ringo. It had been an accident, and Emmy had not meant it. Aunt Charlene had used it sometimes, too, when she had been cross and then felt bad about her behavior.

Ringo turned to look back at the man. He was on his knees in the middle of the empty street, doubled over in pain as if he had been punched in the stomach. He was sobbing like a baby, his face scrunched up with emotion. "I'm sorry," he screamed, over and over. "Sorry! Sorry! Sorry!"

Ringo understood. The man had lost his family, just like Ringo had. He and Ringo would be a new family. Ringo trotted back to the man and stood in front of him. As they faced each other, the man began to talk to him. His voice had that tone that people usually took on when they spoke to dogs. He was asking Ringo a question, which Ringo didn't understand. Then he heard the word "food." Yes, Ringo needed food. And did he hear the word "beach?" Were they going to go to the beach?

The man was letting Ringo sniff him—yes, this was the human that Ringo wanted. The man squatted down and began to pet Ringo. He was crying again, softer this time. Ringo held his body still. The man needed companionship and comfort, and Ringo would give it to him.

* * *

Tobey had never seen a dog like this. He was grey and without fur—as hairless as a baby's bottom, but his skin was covered with spidery lines, more like an elderly person's bottom, and powdered with dry, ashy skin. His egg-shaped body was balanced on four bony legs, and his face was wide in the back, narrow at the nose. Tobey was always more partial to large dogs, or wrinkly ones, or dogs with floppy ears; but this dog did not have any of those qualities—he was small, and his pointy ears stuck up from his head like two triangular tombstones. Tobey thought that he must be a freaky type of mutt, with an unfortunate genetic abnormality, maybe. Because why would anyone ever breed a dog who looked like this? He looked like a fat rat. And to make things even worse, he must have had skin problems at one time. There were circular scars around his butthole and down his back legs, dime-size rings that looked like a bad rash that had since healed into a survivor's souvenir.

What the hell. He was a sweet little thing. He seemed a little dumb and slow to move, although he had no problem gaining ground when Tobey was trying to get him back. This didn't look like a dog who could win competitions, perform fancy tricks, or herd horses. So what? Tobey could relate to the little thing. They were just right for each other. They could be losers together—the big, awkward guy and the small, rat-faced dog. And Tobey was growing to like him. He did seem emotionally intelligent, anyway, and able to understand Tobey's moods. Who in the world forgave a man for the violence Tobey had done to this poor dog? Tobey didn't know, but he would spend the rest of this dog's life making it up to him. For better or worse, Tobey was now the owner of a small, ugly dog. The name etched into the dog's tag was "Ringo." Seemed appropriate enough.

"Welcome to the family, Ringo," Tobey said. They were in the kitchen while Tobey and Ringo both ate meatloaf. His mother had made it and put it in the freezer a couple of weeks ago. Tobey was going to miss her food. And her. And everyone else in the world.

God almighty, life was weird. The Internet was down, maybe permanently. Tobey was not much into social media, anyway, but the phones still worked. Tobey had been on his cell phone all afternoon, calling every relative and friend he could think of: everyone in his contact list, his parents' lists, and Tom's long list. He had even called their old family dentist (they had stopped going to him years ago, after he had raised his rates), and he had called the people who had lived next door ten years ago but still sent holiday cards. No one had answered. And they probably wouldn't call back, Tobey guessed. And the neighbors, the ones who had dropped by early in the plague to check on the family, some he had met for the first time—dead, all of them, most likely. The neighborhood was silent, as still as a desert—no traffic, no voices, no lawn mowers, no dogs barking, even the birds and the crickets were silent. Were they dead, too? *At least I have Ringo*, Tobey thought. Man's best friend. Man's only friend. *Sinabi mo*, as his parents would say. *Ain't it the truth.*

The beach. Tobey had promised Ringo that they would go to the beach. Tobey was still recovering from yesterday's big dig, but he needed to get out of this house. Maybe he would go sleep on the sand, or find an empty motel. He could take his new dog and go find a place to have another good scream and cry.

Ringo had finished his meal. He was lying on the kitchen floor, his head pressed firmly onto Tobey's foot, as if to make sure that Tobey wouldn't go away. Tobey felt his eyes sting with tears as he looked down at Ringo's soft little body. Ringo looked up at Tobey and cocked his head. He looked like he was about to ask a question. What a sensitive, perceptive dog. Was anything wrong, Ringo seemed to ask. *Nothing was wrong*, Tobey thought. He just loved his new dog.

"Want to go to the beach?"

Ringo seemed to understand. He stood up and trotted to the front door.

* * *

The strip used to be a happening place, before the plague. The boardwalk would be crammed with people jogging, skating, and biking; the beach would be carpeted with beach towels and oily bodies, shops and restaurants would be bustling and crowded.

Tobey and Ringo strolled on the boardwalk. Tobey had expected that they would be walking on a deserted beach, like lonely island castaways hoping for rescue, searching the horizon for rescue boats. He was relieved to see other people. This was the kind of crowd that might show up at dawn in the middle of the coldest January day. The lack of a busy summertime scene on a sunny day felt a bit eerie, though. And everyone looked haunted, like recently released war survivors, or so Tobey thought. He had seen so many disaster movies, it was all he could compare this to. They nodded at Tobey and Ringo, or said hello, but not much else.

He had not gone to the strip much when he was growing up; he usually just went with his family when they took visiting relatives. Tobey's family had avoided the tourist areas; they had just gone to the local inlets for picnics and crabbing.

Tobey and his girlfriend, Chelsea, had been regulars at the strip two summers ago. Chelsea the Seashell Girl, he used to call her. Seashell, because she had loved the beach. She had been Tobey's first girlfriend—his only one, so far. Tobey hadn't seen her since that summer, and she had not answered her phone, so Tobey could only assume the worst.

It was a warm June day, a little humid, but tolerable because of a slight, continuous breeze. Jeans and T-shirt weather, not bikini weather, Tobey thought. But girls would have been wearing them anyway, before the plague. BTP.

Ringo had been behaving oddly. Whenever they passed someone, he would run up to the person and sniff his or her legs, then snort, as if he didn't like the smell of the person, and then he would trot back to Tobey. Tobey was puzzled and amused. It was odd behavior, but he was an odd dog. It was almost as if Ringo were checking out other people, then deciding that Tobey was the right guy for him after all. Make up your mind, little dog.

Tobey found his favorite ledge, the spot where he and Chelsea would sit to eat cheese fries and watch people go by. He placed Ringo up on the ledge and then sat next to the dog.

"Chelsea and I used to sit here," he explained to Ringo. "You would have liked her, I hope. But you're kind of picky, aren't you? Well, she was a babe. You'd be lucky if she took you on."

Chelsea had always worn dark, loose clothes that had been too old for her. Tobey had laughed at her swimsuit— black, with a skirt to cover her thighs, as if she had an out-of-shape body that needed to be covered. She definitely did not. She had it all—she was both petite and voluptuous, firm and soft, curvy in all the right places. She had a body that could have rocked a bikini and made every head turn in admiration. She had been gorgeous naked—a wonderland body, like that old song. It was like a delicious secret that Tobey could keep to himself. She had been two and half years older than Tobey, twenty-one to Tobey's eighteen, and Tobey had kidded that she still had a body of a young woman. Then she had moved to San Jose with her parents, met a twenty-nine year-old Google executive, and it was all over for Tobey.

Tobey had spent the next two months raging through Tinder, then holed up his bedroom for a week, feeling dirty, ashamed and lonelier than he'd ever been in his life. A six-month temp assignment had left him madly crushing over a woman two desks over, a forty-year-old Jennifer Aniston look-a-like who had left Tobey panicked and speechless in the aftermath of her gentle sashays down the cubicle aisles. Tobey had a hard time admitting to himself that he was, at heart, an old-fashioned Catholic die-hard, a one-woman man who was wired to be happiest when monogamous. What he really wanted was a woman who was patient and kind, like his mother, or someone who could crack bad puns and dissolve into giggles with his favorite girl cousins, Marisa and Teresa. Rest in peace, ladies.

Chelsea could have been the one, if the timing had been right. Chelsea the Seashell Girl. Tobey formed these words in his brain and savored them. She had a quiet, sweet, cheerful personality. Hanging out with her was like eating a caramel sundae on a warm summer day. Tobey had thought that Chelsea was special, but maybe she wasn't. Girls who were pretty and pleasant were everywhere—before the plague. That was then, this is now. Tobey sighed. At least he had Ringo.

Tobey reached out to pat Ringo on his rump. Ringo was small enough to be a lap dog, but he seemed to prefer sitting next to Tobey and leaning on his thighs, which Tobey liked. He had always thought that lap dogs were for girls. Ringo seemed tired now, and he leaned lazily into Tobey's leg. All that investigation into other human smells was pooping him out, maybe. Perhaps it would be better if he just stayed with his original choice.

"Just stick with me, Ringo," Tobey said. "I'm not letting you go, anyway, no matter who smells better."

A sixty-ish woman with bright purple hair was approaching them. She was wearing a purple jogging suit and neon purple sneakers that matched her hair. Tobey thought that she looked like an eccentric grandma out for her power walk, like someone who didn't realize that the world had gone through a cataclysmic event—why exercise when the world was ending?

"Hello, little one!" She said to Ringo as she approached. "Not you, big guy," she said to Tobey with a grin. She reached out to Ringo and tried to pet him. Ringo yelped in protest, then shimmied backwards and hid his head behind Tobey's back.

"He's a friendly dog," Tobey explained. "But he's kind of tired."

"Has he always been yours?"

"No. I found him yesterday. Well, he found me."

"You're lucky. He seems quite attached to you. Good luck to you. I think that everything will be okay, in the end." That said, the woman walked off, pumping her arms as she sped away.

"There goes a real survivor," Tobey said to Ringo as they watched her walk off. "That lady is determined to be optimistic, wouldn't you say?"

Ringo snorted and pushed the side of his body firmly into Tobey's thigh, as if to say that he preferred Tobey's sad sack ways. Tobey was pleased. This dog could have anyone he wanted, and he wanted Tobey.

"Okay, bud. You stick with me and I'll stick with you," Tobey said. In response, Ringo put his head down on Tobey's lap and looked up at him with soft, loving eyes.

"Ready to go home?"

* * *

Tobey and Ringo were walking back to the car when Ringo lifted his nose and furrowed his face.

"What's that smell, Ringo?" Tobey asked, amused.

Ringo trotted away, appearing to be suddenly energized and excited. Tobey followed him, walking faster and faster as Ringo began to run. Tobey felt worried. Now what? He had not bothered to put a leash on the dog, so maybe now he needed to loot a store and get one?

"Ringo! Get back here!" In the distance Tobey could see Ringo run onto the sand and straight towards a man who was sitting cross-legged on a straw matt. The man's face was lifted up to the sky. A sun-worshiping yoga pose, Tobey thought, or a man just basking in a moment of peace. Ringo was wagging his tail in a frenzied excitement and whimpering; luckily he didn't jump on the man or lick him, he only stood and faced him. Ringo looked as if he was using all the discipline he could muster not to jump all over the man with his happy doggy energy. The man continued to sit still, as if he was unaware of Ringo.

"Sorry about that," Tobey said as he approached them. "My dog seems to like you a lot. Sorry if we interrupted you."

Tobey was a little bit worried that Ringo belonged to the man, or maybe they knew each other? But the man did not seem to know Ringo. No one could forget a dog who looked like Ringo, anyway.

It was obvious that the man had been meditating. He was a thin, leathery man with shaggy grey hair; he looked like someone who meditates, but then again, lots of people did. Chelsea had said it helped her with studying; Tom had gone on a retreat in the Blue Ridge Mountains—he came back willing to pay the money for Tobey to sign up for it, but Tobey had refused. Tobey was not into following Tom's footsteps.

The man opened his eyes and smiled at Tobey. His eyes crinkled with a genuine warmth, a saintly grin that made Tobey think of a skinny Santa with a monkish vibe.

"Not a problem," he said. He glanced at Ringo. "I had two cats, but I love dogs. Especially little ones like this who are survivors." He reached out to pat Ringo on the head. Ringo wagged his tail even harder; the back half of his body whipped back and forth from the force of his tail.

"How are you doing?" the man asked.

Tobey shrugged. "Okay, I guess. Under the circumstances." What do you say to a question like that? *How was he doing?* Before the plague, he had been unemployed, without a girlfriend, and clueless about how to put together an adult life. And did any of that even matter anymore? Now he was just a boy with a dog.

"You're so young," he man said. "This is tough for everyone, but especially the young, I would think. You have to regroup and rebuild. Do you have a place to stay?"

"Yeah, I'm still at home for now," Tobey mumbled. The man's sympathy was too much for Tobey; tears started to form in his eyes and his breath was sucking away from him. Tobey felt an irrational need to get away from this man. He picked up Ringo, who started to squirm in his arms. *You're staying with me, bud*, Tobey thought. *You picked me, and you're staying.*

"See you later," Tobey said as he turned to go.

"I'm here every day," the man said as he closed his eyes and turned his face back up to the sun.

Tobey walked off with Ringo in his arms. Ringo whined and craned his body backwards, gazing at the man with longing eyes. Tobey walked faster, feeling irritated with Ringo.

After they were a safe distance away, Tobey put Ringo down on the ground. "You're my dog, not his," he said.

Ringo spotted the car in the distance and trotted over to it. He sat by it and looked at Tobey expectantly. Time for us to go home, Ringo seemed to say.

"Smart dog," Tobey muttered.

* * *

Ringo settled into his seat, feeling tired but happy. When could they go again? He angled his head out the window so that he could get away from the car odors that mingled with Tobey's warm and sweaty body.

The man on the beach had made Tobey put out vibrations of unease, but Ringo sensed that Tobey was happy now. He was stroking Ringo's backside and talking; Ringo could hear his tones of love and affection. It had been a great afternoon.

Despite all the rotting bodies, the beach smelled healthier and cleaner than it had in Ringo's past outings with Aunt Charlene and Emmy. It was difficult, though, to see that the old human community was gone—only Tobey and that one man were rot free and healthy.

A scent blew into Ringo's nose. What was that? Another healthy human? Ringo lost the scent, so he turned his head to try to find it again. There it was, stronger this time. Ringo wriggled his nose. It smelled like a child, a healthy, disease-free child. A girl child, maybe? Ringo could detect a female body and a feminine vibration. The scent wafted by, and Ringo strained to catch it. Yes—she was a girl. No—she was not a girl. She was a *toddler*. Ringo could hear a voice in the distance.

"Doggy," she said. Her voice was thin and weak.

Ringo barked a few times, then paused.

"Doggy," said the toddler again.

Her scent was stronger now, but Ringo could not see her.

"Nice doggy," she whispered.

She was alone. She was calling him. Ringo began to bark again as Tobey drove off.

Ringo paused. He could no longer hear her or smell her. Where was she? Ringo curled his neck out the window and barked as loud as he could. He turned back to Tobey and barked insistently.

"Quiet!" Tobey yelled.

Ringo stopped barking and lowered his head in submission. Tobey's bad temper was bubbling up, and Ringo didn't want to ruin their nice afternoon.

Part II

As soon as Tobey and Ringo returned home, Ringo jumped out of the car and bolted down the street. Tobey jogged after him, feeling tired and annoyed. Two blocks later, Tobey caught up to his dog—Ringo was shaking and whimpering with excitement as he faced an adolescent girl who was sitting on the front stoop of a house. She didn't pet Ringo, but she appeared unafraid. She raised her hand in a simple wave, like a shy kid in class with a tentative question. Tobey returned the gesture.

"Hey," she said softly. She looked about fourteen. She was tall and slender, and she had long, straight brown hair. She wore jeans, a small straw hat and a denim shirt covered with embroidered cats. She looked like she was ready to assist Martha Stewart in the garden and then go sit under a tree to read some poetry.

"Hey," Tobey said. "Ringo is harmless. He just likes you."

"I've seen you and Ringo around, I think," she said. Her voice was high for a tall girl. "I'm Joni Marigold."

"Hi Joni," Tobey said. He wondered if that were her real name; somehow it just didn't sound real. It certainly would be easy for a girl to take on a new name if she wanted to. It didn't matter—her name seemed to fit her.

Tobey studied her. She must be alone in the world—family, friends, school, cheerleading practice, or whatever it was that she had been into—gone, all gone. She looked more like the type who volunteered in the school library or played the violin. Tobey realized that he had taken in Ringo; now he had to take in Joni Marigold.

"I'm Tobey. Do you want to come see where Ringo and I live?"

Joni nodded. She couldn't say much—her face was scrunched up in silent pain and tears were starting to drip down her face.

* * *

The girl could sleep. Once she got into Tobey's house, she took to the couch and slept for the rest of the day and the next few days; she woke up a few times each day to eat a meal with Tobey, then she slept some more. Joni Marigold seemed more like an old lady than a young one, and Tobey wasn't sure what to make of her lethargy. When awake, she came across as energetic, almost athletic in a graceful way, like a dancer, or maybe a girl who had taken a lot of ballet classes. She reminded Tobey of the cat his family had when he was a kid—languid and still, yet watchful, alert, and able to run and pounce at a moment's notice.

Her energy affected Ringo as well—he joined Joni on the couch and snoozed right along with her. The electricity was still up and running, so Tobey watched movies, played video games and cooked elaborate meals. The neighborhood had a lot of backyard gardens full of vine-ripened vegetables, so Tobey foraged for fresh veggies and made dishes of pasta, tomatoes, zucchini, cheese, and herbs tossed with oil and vinegar. Sometimes he made submarine sandwiches with thick slices of beefsteak tomatoes, or he cooked veggie omelets from eggs he stole from refrigerators. He had never cooked much for his parents and his brother, but they had liked watching cooking shows.

Tobey was surprised at how much he enjoyed it. Eggs, bread, and summer vegetables were going to go bad soon, so he wanted to get those eaten before they were limited to canned food.

Joni seemed to appreciate it all. She would wash the dishes and then state that she would cook next time; then she would go to sleep again, right after every meal.

After a couple of days, Tobey started to spend more time walking around the neighborhood, which had become a ghost town. Even the military men who had gone around gathering dead bodies were gone. Tobey would knock on doors or go straight into homes, looking for bodies to bury, a part of him hoping that he wouldn't find anything. On the third day of this, he did approach a house that had a bad smell. Tobey knew that there was a body—and there it was in the backyard, laying out in a face-up position. There *she* was, dressed in a green gown and fancy jewels, as if to say: "Hello, Tobey. I've been waiting for you. I'm sorry I'm so decomposed, but thank you for finding me."

Tobey couldn't deal with it, with *her*—no, no, no—so he took a blanket out of the house and threw it on top of her, whispered a Hail Mary and then walked away. After that he learned that he just had to use his nose to figure out if a body was in the house. He found a few more bodies, but he couldn't deal with those, either. He would check back later, maybe, after the flies were done and the bodies were dry and more manageable. Is that how it ended? He didn't want to think about it. It was more important to deal with the sleeping beauty at home.

He drove to a grocery store and took home bulk packages of bottled water and cans of soda. He found a gas station that worked, so he spent an afternoon filling up his family's two cars and about ten other cars on his street. Car keys were pretty easy to find in empty houses; most families kept them in their entryway, the kitchen counter, or a purse on a bedroom dresser.

He sometimes just sat and stared at the sleeping girl and the snoring dog and grappled with a growing apprehension. Geez, she was a kid, at the same time she was probably just a handful of years younger than himself. If she was mature, she could help him figure all this out. But maybe not. She could be useless, annoying, and a burden—time would tell. She was also an attractive girl, so maybe someday . . . Tobey put up a wall whenever those thoughts crept in. He mostly felt honored that she seemed to feel so safe and relaxed in his home. It was as if he was her new father now, and she had no worries. Tobey was grateful for the company, but her presence gave him a new kind of anxiety that had not been there when he had been alone.

Joni seemed to have a quiet demeanor; but as each day progressed, she began to talk more and more during her non-sleeping hours—teenage talk about nothing in particular. Her dream had been to go into nursing. Her mother had survived early stage breast cancer, and the time Joni had spent in hospitals left her "one hundred percent sure," she said, that nursing was her calling. She had loved watching the busy nurses, and she had loved being among the staff in the hospital cafeteria. She could pick out who were the doctors, the administrators, or the technicians, or so she thought. She liked the nurses best. She wanted to be one of them; she was sure of that.

Joni loved to remember the "old days," as she called it, and she would talk about the actors she loved (Joaquin Phoenix and Kate Winslet) and the old pop bands from the

1960s that she loved: the Beatles for sure, the Mamas and the Papas; the Beach Boys; and Joni Mitchell, of course, who she was named after. But she didn't like that "loud stuff," from the '60s, as she called it. Tobey had debated that music from Led Zeppelin, The Who, and Jimi Hendrix was superior, but Joni had waved off those bands as "dirty noise." And Bob Dylan, her dad's favorite, was someone she did not get—at all.

It was as if she were catching up on both her sleep and her need for conversation. On the tenth morning, she came into the kitchen looking rested. She had pulled her hair back into a neat ponytail and put on one of Tom's clean T-shirts. She looked sparkly, alert, and ready for a day at school.

"Hey sleepy girl," Tobey said as she glided into the room.

"I think I'm good now," Joni said cheerfully. "I can feel it—it's like I'm all caught up. You know, on my sleep."

"Great," Tobey said politely, but now he felt uncomfortable. What would he do and say to this girl day after day? He had impulsively taken her in, now he wondered if that was the right thing to do. Shouldn't she be hanging out with a woman? Maybe she should live with that woman on the beach, the optimistic power-walker with the purple hair. The one Ringo didn't like. That would make Ringo crazy, Tobey thought, amused. But then he felt anxious again. Tobey sighed. He didn't know what to do with her; hell, he didn't know what to do with himself.

"Do you want to go to the beach today?" he said.

* * *

It was a cool day for summer. Joni had lowered her window just a little, "to keep Ringo from sticking his whole head out," she had explained. She gazed out the window as Tobey drove. Ringo sat in her lap and looked out as well, their heads cocked at a similar angle, like cross-species creatures who were siblings in spirit.

"The grass is getting long," she murmured. "Everything is overgrown now. It's so weird, you know?"

"Yup," Tobey said, trying to appear nonchalant about the changed city.

Tobey grew up in a city that had a manicured middle-class suburban look: subdivisions, office parks, dull strip malls, and shopping malls as the main downtown centers. There had been miles and miles of clean, quiet boulevards, but no places for a pedestrian scene except for malls and the beach. Tobey used to think he would want to go in either direction: a one-store mountain town or New York City, but he never really knew—he had lived here his entire life. And now, looking around, he was homesick for what the city once was.

It was, as Joni said, a weird world now. Median strips were overgrown with long grasses, leaves littered the roads, and the weather, normally so hot and humid at this time of year, was unseasonably cool. Despite the shaggy environment, the air smelled fresh and the sky was streaked with bright clouds—it was as if the gods had recently washed some linen and left it stretched across the sky.

"It's a gorgeous day," Joni mused. "It's amazing what a few weeks without cars on the roads has done for the air. I can't wait to see the beach."

They were alone on the highway; Tobey drove at 75 mph, but it felt like 35. He glanced over to see if Joni was falling asleep, but she looked alert.

"Ringo and I have been to the beach before," Tobey said. "The day that Ringo found you. There were other people there—not many, though. And Ringo was acting weird. He's a funny dog."

"Weird? How so?"

"It's like he was sniffing people out, making judgements. He would smell people and then snort and run away. He only liked this one old guy who was sitting by himself on the sand."

Joni was silent. Tobey glanced at her. She appeared to be thinking about this, her eyebrows pressed together in deep thought.

"And he likes you and me, but that's about it," Tobey added.

"It could be a dog thing."

"How so?"

"Well, I saw a documentary about how dogs can sniff out cancer and other diseases. Do you think he's looking for people who will survive the plague? I mean, maybe that man is healthy too. No virus in him."

"That could be," Tobey said. The lady in the purple hair and clothes had seemed healthy, but Tobey could now recall that she had dark yellow bags under her eyes. He had seen these in his father, mother, and brother in the early stages of their illnesses. The man did not have those bags.

Joni sighed. "Are you happy to be alive? Do you sometimes wish you had died with everyone else?"

"Yes, I think I am happy," Tobey said slowly. "And that's a surprise, but I guess it's just that human will to survive. And I don't want to feel sick or be in pain."

"Yeah, me too."

They were now on a boulevard lined with car lots. The buildings were spray painted with graffiti and the cars looked dusty. A cloud crossed over the sun, creating a brief moment of twilight followed by blinding reflections off a row of Toyotas.

Ringo pressed his nose to the top of the window and whimpered.

"You know, I think you may be right about Ringo," Tobey said.

Maybe," Joni said. "I don't really know what goes on in a dog's head, but I think they know more than we think. They can feel people out. My grandmother believed that. Did you like that man?"

"Yeah, he seemed nice."

"It's so sad to be alone. I was alone. Why didn't you guys join up the way that you and I did?"

"I don't know. We just didn't go there."

They had arrived. Tobey pulled up to an empty motel parking lot.

They walked on to the boardwalk. Unlike last time, the beach was completely empty of life. Tobey saw a few bodies on the sand, corpses sunbathing on a bright summer day. A lone seagull flew overhead. Ringo barked at it. Tobey became aware of how great the acoustics were in this empty world. Ringo's voice sounded as clean as the sky, and the ocean waves sounded majestic, like thousands of drops of sea water working together as an orchestra. It was like the latest high-tech audio experience, the best nature sounds album ever made.

Joni started to sniffle. Tobey sighed. He had thought that she would enjoy this; in reality, it was a heartbreaking shocker.

"I'm sorry," Joni said as she wiped her face. "It's just been so huge."

"Do you want to go back home?"

"No, let's just walk for a while."

Ringo was lifting his nose into the air and sniffing the wind.

"There's someone!" Joni said. She pointed to a figure in the distance. Tobey could barely squint out a human form; but yes, there was someone out there, standing on the sand with his legs wide and his arms stretched out, like a model doing a yoga pose for his beach photo shoot.

Ringo began barking and trotting towards the person, who then turned to face them. As Tobey and Joni ran along with Ringo, the image became clearer. Tobey could see that he was the man from before. Tobey could recognize his short, thin body, his long shaggy hair, his leathery skin, and his dark windbreaker.

"That's the man we were talking about," Tobey said.

He was smiling broadly and waving to them as they approached, looking like a host greeting guests at his party.

"Hello again," he said.

"Hey," Tobey said. He paused to catch his breath. "I don't think we really met last time. I'm Tobey, and this is Joni."

"I'm Rob."

"I was thinking about you," Tobey said.

"You were?" Rob said. He stood still and looked amused while Ringo ran happy circles around him.

"I hope I wasn't short with you last time. I just—to tell you the truth, I thought that the dog I found wanted to leave me and stay with you, and I couldn't handle that."

"And I might have taken him. I've never seen a dog take to me like this before. He's probably just lonely for more people." Rob bent down and began patting Ringo's head. Ringo lifted his nose to Rob, as if to invite a kiss. "What a sweetie," Rob murmured.

"We think that Ringo can smell the disease," Joni said. "He likes people who don't have the bug. And he likes you, so you're probably immune."

"Really? Well. That's something. You may be right. This beach has emptied out, but I'm feeling fine. Did you see that woman with the purple hair last time? I found her body this morning."

Tobey felt a blast of sadness. "That's unfortunate," he said. Now he felt silly, saying that. It was an expression his brother Tom had used when their aunt got sick. Tom had sounded as if he was practicing for when he would be a doctor. Terminal illness? That's unfortunate. Here are your options.

"Let's walk," Rob said, his voice strong and cheerful, as if to get everyone to shake off the melancholy mood. "I've been staying in this big beach house that belonged to a rich family that my wife and I knew. I've stocked it with bottled water and canned food. It's gorgeous. I'll show it to you."

Rob talked as they walked, and Joni was looking at him the way a girl might look at her favorite uncle. Tobey felt relieved. Another man, a grown-up man, might know what to do.

"My wife and I used to own a diner on the strip called The Seaside," Rob said.

"I've been there!" Joni said.

"Me too," Tobey said.

"I waited on tables a lot, because we couldn't afford help. I've probably served you," Rob said. "Then we did what we really wanted to do—we opened a yoga and meditation studio on Virginia Beach Boulevard, but we sold it five years ago, when my wife developed health problems. We still came here a lot, though, because my wife liked it, and she got her exercise that way."

"Did you lose a lot of family, Rob?" Joni said.

"Yes and no. I had always thought of myself as a loner, but this has been ..." his face twisted in pain. "Difficult. I had been taking care of my wife, who had Alzheimer's. I'd been alone a lot, you know, just me dealing with her illness, and she was going fast. Then *this* happened. I've had some phone calls with a cousin in Delaware who has survived this plague so far, so that's good. She's found some friends up there. But this kind of loneliness is something that can even make a man like me go, I don't know. A bit nuts." He laughed then, a one-note bark of hollow humor. "I'm just glad to see you guys."

"It's been hard for everyone," Joni said in a sympathetic nurse-like tone.

A silence hung in the air. Joni wiped at a tear. This was too much for Tobey, who did not want things to dissolve into an emotional group cry.

"We have a theory about Ringo, like we said," Tobey said. "We think he's been trying to find people who will survive the plague."

"He's been sniffing out people," Joni added. "He likes you a lot, so . . ." Joni glanced questioningly at Tobey, who nodded in agreement. "He thinks you might belong with us," Joni said.

"Yes," Tobey said. He felt as if he was in a scene with Dorothy and Toto. Tin Man, would you like to join us on our journey?

"That's interesting," Rob said, his voice tentative. "We could try it out."

"Of course you have to join us," Joni said. "You *can't* be alone." She was saying what Tobey was thinking, but with a woman's touch of graciousness and sympathy. Her face was on the brink of emotion, teardrops on the ledges of her eyes, poised for free fall. What a sweet girl—Chelsea had that same kind of empathy; that's probably why Tobey liked what he knew about Joni so far.

Rob, Joni, Tobey, and Ringo: a post-pandemic alliance of four scared and lonely souls.

* * *

Or would there be more than four? Ringo pointed his nose up into a breeze. Then he ran off, barking furiously. The three humans ran after Ringo, who began trotting faster and faster until he was sprinting at top speed. He was like a dog at the tracks, going for the big win.

"What is he, a greyhound?' Tobey sputtered. He had not sprinted this fast since basketball tryouts his sophomore year. He could hear Rob panting.

"I can't keep up," Rob shouted.

"We'll come back and get you," Tobey said.

By the time Ringo braked to a stop, they had been sprinting for a quarter of a mile, in Tobey's estimation. One fast lap around a track.

Ringo's nose was to the ground now, following a trail. Tobey and Joni watched him as their panting slowed to normal. Rob joined them, and the three humans followed

Ringo off the beach. They were led onto the tourist strip, a stretch of narrow road and wide sidewalks lined with T-shirt shops, salt water taffy stores, and cafes. They entered a souvenir store. Tobey could smell coconut oil and bubble gum.

"Is anybody in here?" Tobey said.

"There!" Joni said.

Two children sat in the corner. A boy sat on the floor with his back to the wall and his knees pulled up to his chin. He had brown skin and a closely cropped afro. He looked about eight years old, and he wore jeans and a striped shirt. A pale blonde and blue-eyed girl sat next to him. She looked about four, and she was wearing pink leggings and a matching pink dress. Her hair was parted neatly into two pigtails and tied with pink ribbons.

The boy stared back at them with large, somber eyes. "She doesn't talk anymore," he said. "And I don't know why. But she can eat and stuff. I don't think she's got the thing. It's just something else, like a trauma."

He pushed his legs down and Ringo hopped into his lap. The boy hugged Ringo tightly and buried his face into Ringo's small body.

"You poor kids!" Joni said. She came forward and pulled the boy, the girl, and Ringo into a group hug. Tobey could see the boy's face perched on Joni's thin shoulder. The child looked so tense and exhausted—his eyes met Tobey's eyes briefly, then glanced away. His eyes watered and his lips quivered, but he did not cry.

"I found her," the boy said. "I've been reading books to her. I was thinking it might help her."

"She will be okay," Rob said. "I think the girl just needs time. Kids can be resilient."

"I've been taking care of her," the boy said, his face defiant and proud.

"And you did such a good job," Joni said.

Ringo hopped out of the boy's lap and went to the girl. He licked her face, gently at first, then with more urgency. She stared at everyone with a blank expression. She seemed nervous, but when Joni picked her up, the girl put her arms around Joni's neck and her body softened.

* * *

They all moved into Rob's adopted beach house. It was large and impressive. Tobey estimated that the entryway alone was the size of his childhood bedroom, and the great room seemed about the size of two living rooms. The space was defined by two major areas, one area was for an outsized sectional couch—so large that each person had space to stretch out, if needed—and the second area was for a rustic dining table that seated twelve. Mapped out around the edges of the great room were zones designed for reading, studying, and one-on-one chats. A couple of acoustic guitars leaned in one corner. A shiny yellow hardwood floor covered the entire space. The bedrooms were upstairs, along with balconies that overlooked the ocean.

The kids' names were Shawn and Pippi. Shawn had given Pippi her name, and she seemed to respond to it. Shawn came up with it from the Pippi Longstocking books that he had been reading to her. "So she can be a super-strong hero, like Pippi, I mean the other Pippi, in the books," Shawn had explained.

He was constantly reading from a collection of books he had taken from the library, classic kid stuff like Pippi

Longstocking and Harry Potter, but also a series of biographies of people like Benjamin Franklin, Abe Lincoln and Jackie Robinson. He sometimes read aloud, his voice low and smooth, sounding like a Morgan Freeman narration. Pippi and Ringo would sit across from him, looking alert and engaged.

He liked to pretend that he was an anchorman. He would stand behind the dining table and read old magazines to a pretend camera, his face professional and somber. Rob would point the remote control at Shawn, then Shawn would "change channels" and do something else. He liked to pretend that he was Don Lemon, his favorite CNN newsman, or Walter Smith, the local news anchor. What kid that age liked Walter Smith? Tobey was impressed.

They were a good group. Shawn was a smart kid, destined for journalism, Tobey thought, if the world had not changed. Joni relieved Shawn of his original job and took on the role of Pippi's caretaker. Joni bathed and dressed Pippi each morning, and she gave Pippi a constant, patient attention that Tobey found remarkable. Pippi appeared to be listening to Joni and observing everyone, so that was good, Tobey thought. Like Rob said, she should come out of it. Rob took on the role of playground director, social worker, and morale officer. There was something about Rob's personality that demanded a good attitude and polite behavior, so Tobey put on a cheerful demeanor along with everyone else.

But Tobey was stressed and worried about his new family. Everyone seemed to assume that Tobey was their leader, and it was his job to supervise anything that wasn't fun, like cooking meals, assigning cleanup chores and making the big decisions. It was as if they were waiting for him to figure everything out, and Tobey wasn't sure he wanted this role. Why him? Rob was the oldest, he should take the lead and be the church elder of this group. Tobey could cut out, couldn't he? Leave this scene and be on his own. Take Ringo and go back home—except Ringo didn't want to go home; he spent all his time playing with everyone else while Tobey sat on the sectional and worried.

* * *

Then one day, a week into their new home, Tobey woke up in a mood that he just couldn't shake off. If his father were still around, it would be pick-a-fight time, or hide-in-his-room time. Leave-me-the-eff-alone time—I want to be alone with my Internet and my video games. Tobey missed those days. These kids, these people—who needed it? But Tobey tried to hide it. They were, after all, not his family, and they might not understand his moods.

Tobey was sulking on the sectional that morning when he heard loud wailing upstairs, like a baby who needed to be changed and fed. What the hell?

Joni came downstairs. "Pippi has been crying," she said.

Shawn looked up from his book. He was in a recliner in the far corner of the room. "She's done that before," Shawn said. "But she stops after a while, like ten minutes."

"What should we do?" Joni said to Tobey.

Tobey shrugged, feeling irritated. How would he know more than Joni would know? She was the one who was spending all her time with the girl.

An hour later Pippi was still screaming. Ringo started to bark along with Pippi's crying, endless dog yapping along with endless baby wailing. Ringo had never been much of a barker, as far as Tobey knew. Was he just echoing Pippi's mood or was there something in the air that bothered the both of them?

Tobey was exhausted. All this worry and strain, and now this. What was he supposed to do? He just didn't feel like dealing with it.

Rob trotted down the stairs. "Good morning all. I need to go for a walk on the beach," he said.

Shawn looked up from his book. "I'll go with you," he said.

Rob smiled at Shawn. "This is my walk. I need to be on my own. We'll walk later, okay bud?"

"Whatever," Shawn said as he bent his head back into his book.

While Rob was out, Pippi continued to cry and Ringo continued to bark.

Then Shawn began to complain that he was bored. Tobey reluctantly played Scrabble with Shawn to try to get him to cheer up. Shawn used a word, "zephyr," that Tobey had never heard of, but Tobey did not want to challenge a kid on this and make himself look stupid. Tobey lost the game—a real loss, which left Tobey feeling surprised and aggravated. Shawn wanted to play again, but Tobey did not.

"That was boring, anyway," Shawn said. He flopped into the corner recliner to bury himself in yet another book. Tobey heard Shawn talking to himself. "Sore loser," Shawn muttered. Tobey had a flash of anger. What an arrogant kid.

The crying and the barking continued for another half hour; then came to a sudden stop. *Lovely silence*, Tobey thought. *Finally.*

The lights flickered out—no power, probably forever. It was an amazing mystery that they had it for this long.

Joni came downstairs, looking distraught. "She's asleep now," she said to Tobey. "And she seems okay. But *you* deal with it next time."

Tobey shrugged. So he gets time with Pippi only when she's unpleasant? That was irritating.

"We need to figure it out, Tobey," Joni said. "She's been traumatized, and I'm worried that she won't recover. What do we do?"

"I don't know," Tobey said morosely.

"And the water I've been using to bathe her has been smelling funny. We can't use bottled water for everything. We're going to run out, you know?"

Tobey was silent.

"The tap water doesn't just smell bad—it's brown," Shawn shouted from his corner recliner. "I was just in the bathroom."

Joni said nothing; she just glared at Tobey.

Rob came in the front entry, looking tired but refreshed. His face was flushed with a post-walk glow. "It's nice and cool out," he said.

"I want to go swimming," Shawn said. "Take me!"

"It's about to rain, so you can't," Rob said.

"And the surf is too rough," Tobey said.

"I'm going to take a nap," Rob said. He headed upstairs.

"I want to go swimming!" Shawn yelled. He got up and headed to the front door.

Tobey felt a sudden surge of hot, insane anger. "Well, you can't, alright? The waves are rough and you're just a little kid who can't swim! So sit down and stop being a brat!"

"You're not my dad! My dad didn't yell at me like that! Who are you? Just a big dumb gorilla king kong. You can't even beat a little kid at Scrabble." Shawn started to head out the door.

Tobey was furious. "Get back here!" he yelled. Tobey went to Shawn, picked up the angry child, and tossed him on the sectional. He loomed down at Shawn from above. He wanted to hit the kid, or punch a wall, or go out and scream at the ocean. Why did he survive this thing? Why him? He should have died. Tom should lead these people, not big, stupid Tobey.

"Don't hit me!" Shawn screamed.

Tobey gasped. Shawn's hands were covering his face, and his little body was shaking. He was crying now. *He was crying.* This terrific little kid, who had refused to dissolve into tears when the adults showed up, who had found the skills to take care of a little girl—feed her, bathe her, change her clothes and fix her hair—this kid, who had probably been a leader on the playground and the winner of every spelling bee . . . he had a family, once. And now he had no one. Certainly Tobey could not be relied on.

Rob had come back downstairs. He was staring at Tobey, his face sympathetic. "Let's go take a walk," he said to Tobey.

"Can't. It's raining. You just said so."

"Come on," Rob said. "We need to talk, Big Guy. Now."

Big Guy, Big Toe. There it was again. Tobey sighed. "Let's go," he said to Rob.

* * *

So they walked. The desolate boardwalk was now spiked with long grasses that grew through the cracks. The misty, sprinkling air was under a solid grey sky; the surf was loud and rough. Tobey thought he saw surfers in the distance, black wetsuits racing in on black surf boards—no, they were just mirages, mystery shapes in the murky surf.

Tobey had been feeling both restless and tired, and he didn't know what he needed—exercise, or sleep, or something that he couldn't name. He didn't know what.

"I'm sorry about what I did to Shawn," Tobey admitted. His foul mood was beginning to ebb—he sincerely regretted his outburst, and Rob's calming presence was powerful. "It's just been frustrating. I feel like everybody is looking to me. What do I know? I mean, you're the oldest one here. I'm just a twenty-year-old kid. I was living with my parents when all this happened."

"Are you aware of how old I am?"

"No."

"I'm seventy-eight, and I have a birthday next month."

"Oh."

"And it may not seem so to you, but I do have health issues. I had heart surgery ten years ago. I have high cholesterol and pre-diabetes. My medication has run out, so now I'm living without it. I'm feeling fine now, but I really don't think I should lead this group. I'm a small, old man. You're a tall young man, and there is something about height that makes people assign leadership. Don't you think? I'm sure you've experienced that."

"Not really. I was a dork in high school. I may look like a leader, but I'm not. Sometimes I think I just want to pick up my dog and go out on my own."

"Well, you certainly could do that," Rob said. "No one is stopping you."

But Tobey knew that he could not do that. For one thing, Ringo might not even want to go with him. He tried to imagine the life. He could wander the empty streets all by himself, drinking soda and beer and eating canned food and Oreos. Spam on crackers, day after day. No one to annoy him, no one to talk to—day after day, year and after year. Wandering through the city like a lost, lonely ghost.

"You're aware that I once owned a yoga and meditation studio," Rob said. "I can teach you what I know. I should have thought of this before. There are ways that you can control your temper and stabilize your moods. I can give you some books I've read on how to be an effective leader with a positive vision. I've got parenting books, and books about keeping yourself whole and centered, stuff like that. We can go to my old house and get them. You need to grow up, Tobey. But you can do it, and you don't have to exhaust yourself over it. I will mentor you, and Joni will be a great help. She's got great potential, too. You're a good guy. You can do this."

Tobey stared at the ocean thoughtfully, realizing that the job was his—in a way he had a choice, in a way he did not, but either way the job was his. He could be good at it, or he could be bad at it. He wanted to be good at it.

* * *

"I called this meeting because I've been doing a lot of thinking, and I have a suggestion," Tobey said. It was 10:00 a.m., two days after that really bad day, and everyone had calmed down. They were all seated at the dining table. Tobey thought they looked a bit like a family at Thanksgiving dinner, and he was about to say grace. Except there was no food; maybe it was more like a meeting of executives around a boardroom table.

All heads turned to him. Tobey felt a bit silly. They gave him encouraging smiles, as though they were parents about to hear their child give a speech.

"First of all, I want to apologize to everyone again, especially Shawn, for my bad behavior. I have struggled in the past with controlling my temper, and I don't want to be that way anymore. So, if I ever do that again, feel free to tell me to go away. It will be hard for me, because I've grown to like you guys a lot. In fact, I want to adopt Shawn and Pippi, if they will have me. So does Joni. Rob has agreed to perform the *official* adoption ceremony. We'll do it once we get settled into our next new home."

Shawn put his hand to his mouth and started to giggle. "Sorry," he said. "Ringo is licking my feet."

Tobey had apologized to Shawn in a private conversation. Shawn had shrugged it off, but Tobey did not feel truly forgiven until after they had spent an afternoon playing catch on the beach.

Tobey checked his notes and continued with his speech. "I think that we should move to Florida. I had an uncle who had a big house down there. He had a few acres of land with a lot of fruit trees, some chickens, and a well. And if that doesn't work, we can easily find some other house in that area. Winter is coming to Virginia soon, and I think a tropical environment would be better for us. I found an RV with a tank full of gas, but we will need to put bikes in it in case we need them. We can stock it with some water and food, but we will have to pick up a lot of food along the way. I've mapped out a route with lots of stops in cities and towns. We're lucky that someone in this house had collected old road maps. Rob and Joni and I will be talking more about logistics."

Shawn was pouting. "Pippi and I aren't going," he said. "I want to stay here with my mom and dad. My *original* mom and dad."

Tobey felt frustrated. Shawn had been in good spirits all morning, why was he being difficult now? Tobey took a breath and thought for a moment, as Rob had taught him. "Do you remember where you used to live? We can go back so you can get some things that belonged to your parents."

"Yeah, on 150 Covey Street, in Timber Springs," Shawn said, looking doubtful. "That's C-O-V-E-Y."

"So we can go there. But your parents aren't there anymore, Shawn," Tobey said. "They're up in the sky. So no matter where we live, you can always look up to the clouds and know that your parents are with you."

"Great idea," Rob said. "We should all go home and get photographs and stuff like that. I'll drive the kids. There's a local road map in that drawer with all the others. I'll find Shawn's house. And you and Joni can go back to your old neighborhood. When should we be back, Tobey?"

"Three at the latest. Then we will need to start packing up."

Rob stood up. "Come on, Shawn. Let's go to Covey Street. How did you spell that?"

Shawn laughed as he ran for the front door. "Florida!" he said. "I want oranges! Come on, Pippi!"

After they left, Tobey turned to Joni, who was looking doubtful.

"I didn't want Shawn to get too excited about it yet, but there's more news," he said. "Rob has been in touch with his cousin in Delaware and her survivor friends, and someone in that group found a relative in Chicago and more survivors, and Chicago found people in Minnesota. Rob and I have gotten in touch everyone, and we've all agreed to head down to this area in Florida. People's cell phones are shutting down, so it happened just in time. It's about fifty people, including us."

Joni's face brightened. "That's good," she said. "But I want us to stay together as a family."

"I want that too. That's why it's important that we have that ceremony to adopt Shawn and Pippi. Here's the best part—the Chicago group has kids, and Delaware just found a couple of cats. And each group has at least one dog that helped them find each other, just like Ringo did for us."

"So we couldn't have done this without dogs?"

"Yeah, it seems so."

Joni grinned. "That is so awesome."

* * *

That night, Tobey lay in bed and stared at the ceiling, his thoughts restless. Was this a dream or was he really leading a group of strangers out to a distant state? He was scared—is this what fatherhood was like? No wonder his father was always stressed out.

He tried to still his mind. This meditation stuff was difficult; but sometimes he could get his mind to settle down into a quieter state for a minute or two. His window was wide open. The full moon was casting a soft light into his room, and he could hear the surf. It was gentle tonight. A thought popped into Tobey's head: "Turn the tide of your thoughts in the direction you want to go." That was from a book of seaside poems that Chelsea had given him, one of his keepsakes that would go with him to Florida.

His door creaked open. Tobey could see a slim figure in the doorway. Joni.

"I heard you moving around before," she said. "Are you having trouble sleeping?"

"A little," Tobey said.

Joni walked in and climbed into Tobey's bed. She cuddled into Tobey's body like a wife spooning her husband.

Tobey froze, unable to get himself to move away. He could feel her breasts pressing into his back, her legs pushing into his. Was she just being affectionate or was this something more?

"Do you want to see my breasts?" Joni whispered.

Tobey hopped out of the bed and faced the window. His face was hot, so the soft breeze coming in felt nice. He could feel his body shifting, a readiness beginning to prime him. Sure, he wanted it. Wanted her.

"Haven't you thought about it?" Joni said.

"Of course I have. I think you're amazing."

Of course he had thought about it. About her. He had definitely noticed her sweet ways, her graceful moves, her perky breasts, and the way her body curved from a narrow waist to a sweet, firm rear end. Her hair was long and shiny; her feet, small and delicate. She had kept her toes well-manicured and done up in a rose-colored polish. She had taken to wearing a diamond necklace and bracelets around the house, which she took off when she swam in the ocean. She was the most beautiful woman in the world. Girl. She was a beautiful girl. She wasn't even old enough to be Pippi's biological mother.

"Doesn't it seem obvious that we should re-populate the planet?" she said.

Tobey turned and faced Joni. "How old are you?"

"Sixteen."

"Seriously? I thought you were fourteen or fifteen."

"And I'll be seventeen in two months. And would it matter? It's not like you could get arrested or that I have plans to go to college. And I really do like you, Tobey. Actually, I think I love you."

Tobey took a breath. "Let's wait a while," he said. "We lived in the same neighborhood but in completely different worlds just, what's it been now—about six weeks ago. You have a crush on me because I'm the one guy around who is close to your age. Give it six months. You could meet a guy in Florida, and then you'd forget about me, and I would hate that. We need to figure stuff out first."

Joni smiled. "Okay. But it's not a crush. Six months. I'll check in with you on New Year's Eve."

"You do that," Tobey said.

Joni left, and Tobey stayed at the window and stared at the moonlight on the ceiling. Tobey glanced over at a photo that was propped up on the bedside table. His family. What would Dad do? He would tell Tobey to do the right thing. Tobey took a deep breath, then returned to his bed.

* * *

The smell of distant corpses occasionally blew into Ringo's nose, but that was beginning to go away. These days, Ringo smelled a fresh, fragrant ocean and a clean sky, unadulterated by pollution.

The air was windy that day, but there was a pleasant warmth between the cooling breezes. Everyone was standing outside of the house and getting ready to go into a big, box-like car. Ringo was excited. He loved going on trips, and this seemed as if it would be a big one. What was happening? Everyone was putting out vibes of both eagerness and caution, but mostly Ringo could feel a united determination to cooperate and to make a project work. They were a group on the move, ready for a new phase.

Shawn had been anxious in the past day or so, but today his energy was the happiest of them all. He was jumping up and down and shouting. Ringo heard the word "shotgun." Ringo knew what this meant; Shawn wanted the seat next to the driver. This was terrific—Shawn had taken to hogging all of Ringo's attention, which the group allowed. Ringo had grown to love them all equally, but Shawn needed Ringo for now. And so this meant that Ringo would also sit shotgun, on Shawn's lap.

Joni and Pippi climbed in first. Ringo could sense Joni's mixed emotions: anxiety, sadness, and also some delight. There was a joyful tension simmering between Joni and Tobey, a man-woman kind of energy. It had been there when Joni first appeared at Tobey's house, but it was growing now.

Pippi was doing much better, but the people weren't aware of this. She was becoming less tense and more confident. Pippi's brain was forming words, and her mouth was whispering them. They couldn't hear it, but Ringo could, and Ringo sensed that Pippi's buried personality— goofy, stumbling, playful, and sweet—would soon emerge from her protective walls.

Rob was doing well, too. His lonely existence had been replaced by a strong will to survive. His body, which had been getting weaker, and his blood chemistry, which had been smelling less healthy, were quieted by Rob's robust spirit.

They all settled into their seats, and Tobey started the vehicle. Ringo was most proud of this young man. Tobey was settling down and getting stronger, softer, more confident in his body, and clearer in his thoughts. His seed of decency was being watered, and the good stuff was expanding more and more each day. He was determined to do well in his new role, and his emotional growth was quite impressive.

Ringo shifted around on Shawn's lap as he tried to find a more comfortable position. Pippi's scent was blended with a lavender lotion that filled the car, so Ringo stuck his nose out the window to find other scents. As the car started to accelerate down the street, Ringo could detect back notes of something floral behind the salty ocean. Ringo wiggled his nose in appreciation as the fragrance wafted away. That was lovely.

Ringo felt so happy. Humans had superior brains, he knew that, but he had his own small job to do. They were a pack now, a healthy, cooperative, productive pack. He had done his job. There was more work to do, but today he would relax and enjoy the ride.

Tobey put on some music. Ringo recognized the harmony of voices—the *Beatles*? That recording was from Aunt Charlene's car! She had played this all the time! How did they get this? Then everyone started to sing along. They knew this music too?

"Eight Days a Week . . . I loooove you," they sang. Puzzled but happy, Ringo sang along with his new family.

~ ~ ~

This novella is included in
Stories in the Okay Future, an anthology of short fiction by
C.C. Alma.

An Excerpt From
Stories in the Okay Future

ROBOTS IN LOVE

Three young co-workers munched on tortilla chips and did their usual lunchtime talk: office gossip and complaints about management. Noralyn's morning had been a bad one, for a whole lot of reasons. As usual, Patti Wilson had them laughing.

"You make our bad jobs seem not so bad," Melissa said with a sigh.

"Don't say that. I feel an inspirational Oprah Winfrey quote coming over me," Patti said. "Either her or Susan B. Anthony. Two of the greatest women in history—"

"We know, we know," Melissa said. She rolled her eyes. "A week can't go by without a history quote from you. These new historical holograms have been making people nuts. I wish I had never showed my grandmother how to use it. She's been getting advice from the Oprah hologram, and it's been driving me crazy. Change the subject, quick."

So Patti told a funny story about when she was in the third grade.

"You must have been bullied," Noralyn said sympathetically.

"Nori!" Melissa shrieked, her face reddening.

Noralyn's eyes fluttered downwards and her face also turned red. "Sorry," she muttered.

Patti shrugged. "It's no big deal, guys. Actually, I was not."

Noralyn and Melissa looked surprised. "Of course," Melissa said. "You're so funny, the kids must have loved you!"

"I could make 'em pee in their pants, I was so hilarious," Patti said.

It was the first time Patti's co-workers had said anything about her unfortunate looks. Patti could even forget about it, sometimes, at least when she was with friends. On her first day of work, two years ago, she had been aware of people pulling back from her and carefully controlling their expressions. That's what everyone did when they met her, but meeting a bunch of new people in one day was always difficult. Patti thought her coworkers were used to her by now—seeing only her pretty *insides*—maybe they weren't, maybe that never really happened.

That night, Patti stared at herself in her bathroom mirror. She had come to terms with it, or so she had thought. She was ugly. A harsh word, but it was the only word for it. Her looks weren't so off-the-mark that she was deformed—that might have been better. No, she was just ugly, and her mother had not been able to pay for the needed beauty procedures. They would have been so extensive, anyway, and where do you start? She had one eye that was larger than the other and slightly higher. She had a sharp, pointy nose, low on the face and way too close to her mouth. Her thin lips barely

An Excerpt From
Stories in the Okay Future

ROBOTS IN LOVE

covered her buck teeth. Acne. Patti sighed. Yup, she had it all. Her back was hunched over and crooked. Her breasts were big, but not nicely so. They were heavy and droopy, and they rested on a protruding tummy. What twenty-one-year-old girl had such heavy, saggy boobs? Somehow, Patti did. Even her hands were strange; they were too small for her body, while her feet were way too large. And a frizzy bush of mud-colored hair topped it all. No girlfriend had even offered to fix her hair or give make-up advice. It wouldn't help much.

She hadn't been beat up in school, but she had been teased. Kids try to be funny; they try to make everyone laugh, and Patti had laughed along with them. They called her Old Troll, Ratty Patti, and Reepo, short for repulsive. Of course it hurt.

In the seventh grade, Patti did an oral report on Susan B. Anthony.

"You look a little like her, but uglier," one kid had said to her on the bus later that day. He sounded kind, as if trying to be helpful.

"Oh god! Shut up, Jimmy," retorted a girl from across the aisle.

"But about a hundred times uglier," muttered another kid.

Patti's strength came from her energetic and kind-hearted mother, the only family Patti ever knew. But when Patti had been eighteen, her mom had developed cancer and died.

* * *

That was Patti's work life and her childhood, but soon she was at the end of her short life.

"You have advanced cancer," the doctor said. It was the same cancer that had killed Patti's mom.

She wasn't surprised. Her bones had ached, her lungs had hurt, and she was always waking up exhausted, even after a ten-hour sleep. Then she had found a lump on her underarm—bigger than a pea, smaller than a golf ball. By the time she went to a doctor, it was too late.

She went through it all—anger, denial, bargaining, acceptance. She moved into a hospice. She was only twenty-two years old.

"There's a boy here who is about your age," one of the nurses told Patti. "I think you'd like each other."

As soon as Patti met Peter Bhimjee, she knew why the nurse had said that. He was hideous, just like her. He was fat and prematurely bald, and his head shone in the overhead lighting like a bare lightbulb. He had irregular features, gapped teeth, and chubby hands. He was funny and sweet, just like Patti. He had a wide, shy smile that changed his whole face.

They were so much alike. Peter admired Oprah Winfrey, too, and Ben Franklin. They had read all the same biographies and played with the same historical holograms. They sat next to each other in the cafeteria and talked about their heroes or complained about the

An Excerpt From
Stories in the Okay Future

ROBOTS IN LOVE

hospice staff, just like Patti used to do with her co-workers.

The nurses wheeled Patti into Peter's room every morning. Day after day, Patti and Peter talked about everything they could think of, trying to get to know each other as quickly as they could. One morning they sat in Peter's room and talked about their mutual curse.

"Did you ever wish you were handsome?" Patti said. She sat at a small round table by the window, watching a goldfish swim back and forth in its little bowl.

Peter was stretched out on his bed. He fixed his large brown eyes on Patti. *They're his best feature*, Patti thought with a smile. Suddenly his eyes watered and Patti wished she had never brought it up.

"When I found out I was going to die, I was almost relieved," he admitted. "It never bothered me that I was ugly. I had friends and a busy life. It was just knowing that I would probably live out my life and never have a relationship. I don't blame women. It's unrealistic to expect anyone to be attracted to me." His eyes flickered over to the window. "But then I think, if I could have just gotten to old age. Then it wouldn't matter anymore. When you're ninety-five, no one knows if you were handsome or horrible when you were young."

Patti sighed. He was always so earnest like that, always giving answers that were honest and carefully thought out.

Peter smiled at Patti—that wide, shy smile that she had grown to like so much. "I do have some good features," he said. "My pinky toes are kinda sexy."

That struck them as so funny, a nurse had to ask them to be quiet. They only laughed harder, like two kids in a classroom who couldn't control their giggles.

* * *

Patti couldn't sleep that night. She had been at the hospice for two weeks, and it was the first night that she felt pain-free and comfortable in her body. But she couldn't enjoy it; her thoughts flew around in her brain like restless bees, buzzing about Peter, around and around.

"This? Seriously, God?" Patti's pleading prayer was so intense, she wondered if she had spoken aloud. She stared at the ceiling. "Really, God?" she whispered. "Now, at the end of my short life, you put me through this torture?"

She couldn't deny it anymore. She loved Peter with all her heart and soul. Pleading with God wasn't going to help. Eventually, she slept. When she woke in the morning, she felt a peaceful resolve. "I found love, a real love, finally, at the end of my life," she whispered to the ceiling.

Right after the nurse wheeled Patti into Peter's room for their day together, Patti made herself say it.

An Excerpt From
Stories in the Okay Future

ROBOTS IN LOVE

"We don't have a lot of time left. And I just want to say that—" she stopped, catching a sob in her throat . . .

~ ~ ~

This short story continues in
Stories in the Okay Future, an anthology of short fiction by
C.C. Alma.

ABOUT THE AUTHOR

I hope you enjoyed my novella. I live in Northern California, although I grew up in Virginia Beach, Virginia. I spend my time working as an assistant at a nonprofit, writing fiction, cooking big meals in my small kitchen, struggling through yoga poses, and hanging out with family and friends. I have a B.A. from Old Dominion University; I have also completed several courses in writing and editing at U.C. Berkeley Extension.

I am not great at promotion, but I do care about my readers and hope to continue to find people who would enjoy my stories. If you like this book, it would be helpful if you give me a rating, write a review, or tell your friends about it. Thank you!

~ C.C. Alma ~

Made in the USA
Las Vegas, NV
31 July 2021